ABOUT THE BANK STREET READY-TO-READ SERIES

More than seventy-five years of educational research, innovative teaching, and quality publishing have earned The Bank Street College of Education its reputation as America's most trusted name in early childhood education.

Because no two children are exactly alike in their development, the Bank Street Ready-to-Read series is written on three levels to accommodate the individual stages of reading readiness of children ages three through eight.

○ *Level 1:* **GETTING READY TO READ (Pre-K–Grade 1)**
Level 1 books are perfect for reading aloud with children who are getting ready to read or just starting to read words or phrases. These books feature large type, repetition, and simple sentences.

● *Level 2:* **READING TOGETHER (Grades 1–3)**
These books have slightly smaller type and longer sentences. They are ideal for children beginning to read by themselves who may need help.

○ *Level 3:* **I CAN READ IT MYSELF (Grades 2–3)**
These stories are just right for children who can read independently. They offer more complex and challenging stories and sentences.

All three levels of The Bank Street Ready-to-Read books make it easy to select the books most appropriate for your child's development and enable him or her to grow with the series step by step. The levels purposely overlap to reinforce skills and further encourage reading.

We feel that making reading fun is the single most important thing anyone can do to help children become good readers. We hope you will become part of Bank Street's long tradition of learning through sharing.

The Bank Street College of Education

For Julie
— B.B.

To Jono, gift of God
— N.W.

Please visit our web site at: **www.garethstevens.com**
For a free color catalog describing Gareth Stevens' list of high-quality books and
multimedia programs, call 1-800-542-2595 (USA) or 1-800-461-9120 (Canada).
Gareth Stevens Publishing's Fax: (414) 332-3567.

Library of Congress Cataloging-in-Publication Data

Boegehold, Betty Virginia Doyle.
 A horse called Starfire / by Betty D. Boegehold; illustrated by Neil Waldman.
  p. cm. -- (Bank Street ready-to-read)
 Summary: While hunting with his father, Wolf Cub encounters a horse for the first time.
 ISBN 0-8368-1763-X (lib. bdg.)
 [1. Horses--Fiction. 2. Indians of North America--Fiction.] I. Waldman, Neil, ill.
 II. Title. III. Series.
 PZ7.B63572Ho 1998
 [E]--dc21   97-28917

This edition first published in 1998 by
Gareth Stevens Publishing
A World Almanac Education Group Company
330 West Olive Street, Suite 100
Milwaukee, Wisconsin 53212 USA

Printed in Mexico

2 3 4 5 6 7 8 9 05 04 03 02 01

Bank Street Ready-to-Read™

A Horse Called Starfire

by Betty D. Boegehold
Illustrated by Neil Waldman

A Byron Preiss Book

Gareth Stevens Publishing
A WORLD ALMANAC EDUCATION GROUP COMPANY

Contents

Chapter 1
FROM SPAIN

The man from Spain
called his horse Estrella.
She was a golden horse
with a white star
in the middle of her forehead.

Estrella and the man crossed the ocean
on a crowded sailing boat.
They came all the way from Spain
to the New World,
where there were no horses.

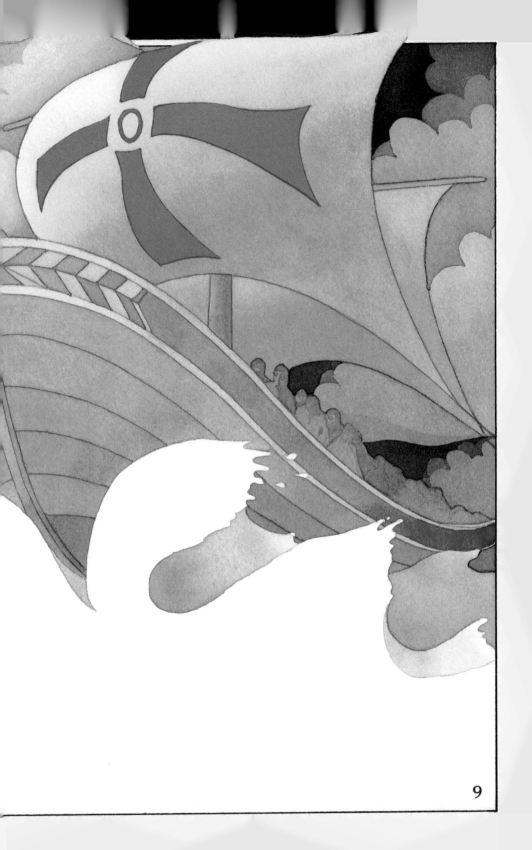

With many other men
and many other horses,
Estrella and her man
set out to explore.

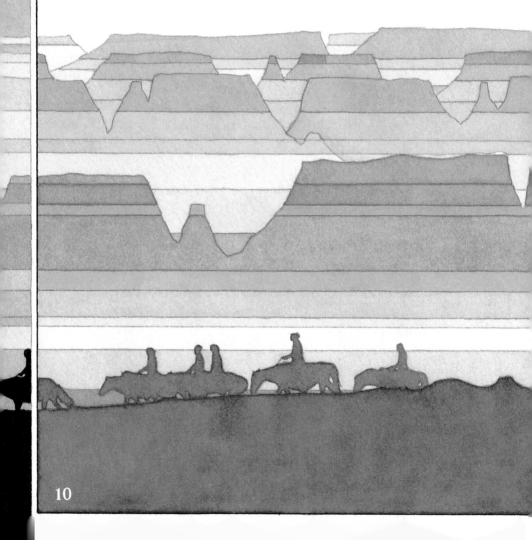

They rode across the new land,
for weeks and weeks.
One day, Estrella's man grew sick.
He fell behind the others
and lost his way.

The man knew he was dying.
"I must free Estrella," he said.
He pulled the saddle and bridle
off the golden horse.

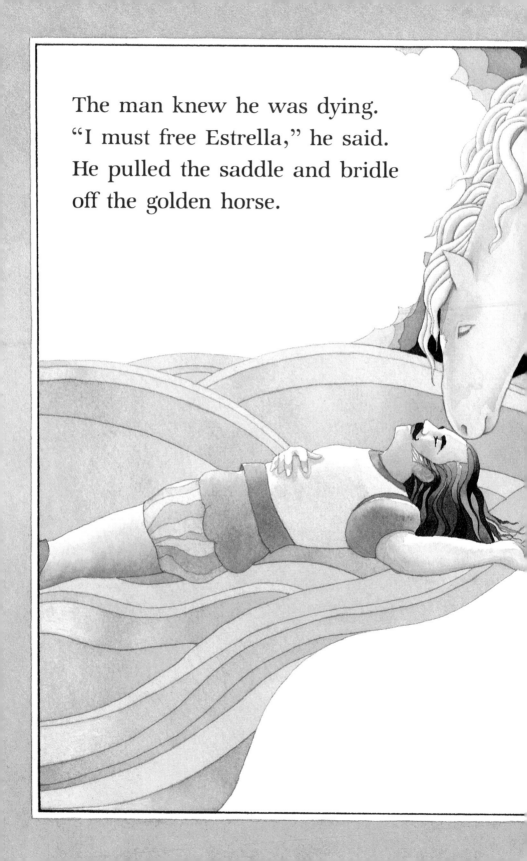

Chapter 2
WOLF CUB

Estrella stayed by her man
all day and all night.
But he did not move.
Somehow the horse knew
he would never move again.

Now Estrella was alone
for the first time in her life.
Alone and hungry,
the golden horse moved away
toward a hill
with a patch of dried grass.

Behind that hill Lone Owl stood
with his son Wolf Cub.
It was Wolf Cub's first hunting trip.
He had dreamed for weeks
of returning to camp
with plenty of big game.
But they had hunted all day,
and had taken only
a few small rabbits.

Lone Owl was ready to go home.
"Father," said Wolf Cub,
"let's stay a little longer.
Maybe our luck will change."

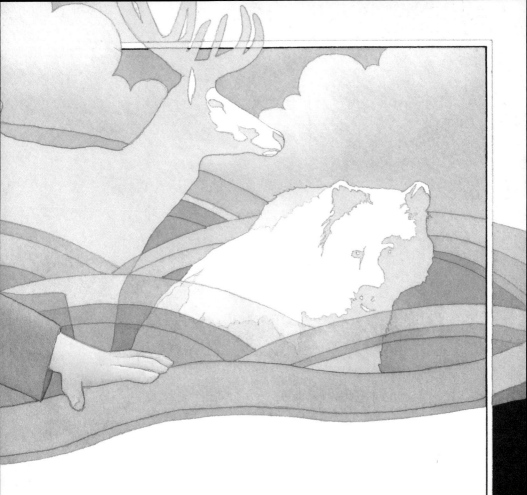

Just then they heard something.
Wolf Cub put his ear to the ground.
Yes. It was a big animal,
moving slowly over the hill.

Was it a deer?
Or maybe a bear?
The two hunters waited
with bows and arrows ready.

Chapter 3
A HORSE

"Remember to ask the animal to forgive us," said Lone Owl. "We must always ask this before taking an animal's life."

Then over the hill came Estrella.
Wolf Cub could not believe his eyes.
He had never seen an animal
like this one.
"Father," he whispered, "what is it?"

"Don't move," said Lone Owl.
Estrella lifted her head.
She sniffed the air
and looked straight at them.
Then she moved down the hill.

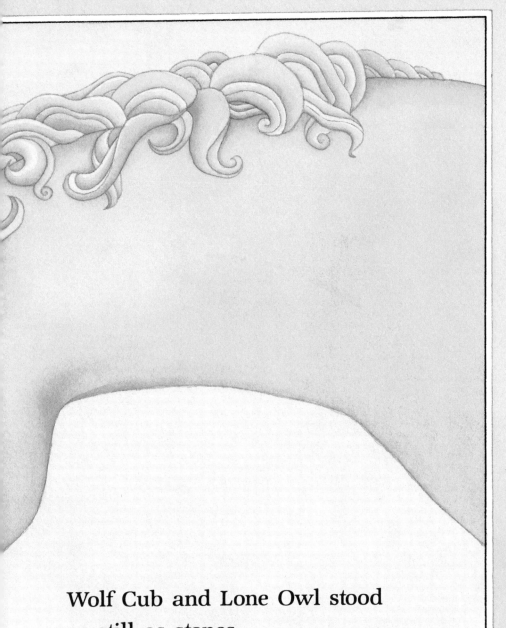

Wolf Cub and Lone Owl stood
as still as stones.
Estrella walked up to Wolf Cub.
She stopped and bent her head
and softly touched his arm.

The boy was filled with wonder.
This strange animal was not afraid
of him. Slowly he lifted his hand
and patted the animal on the nose.

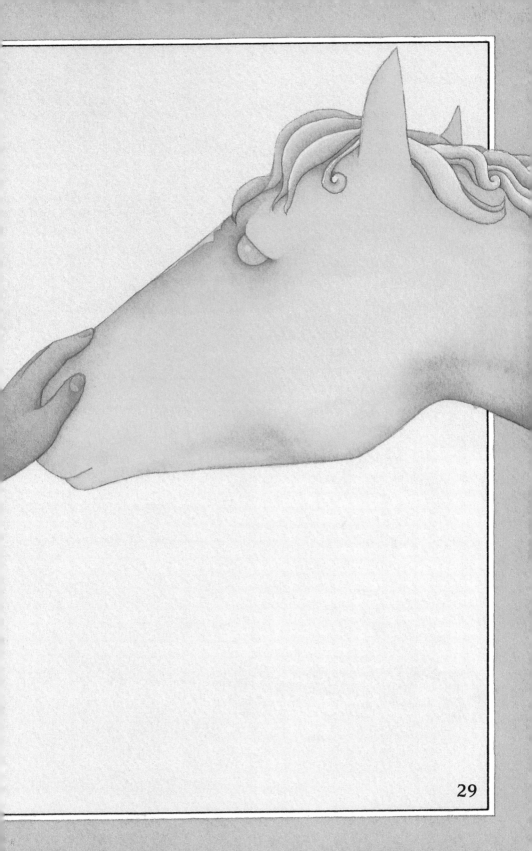

30

"Father, this is not a wild animal,"
he said.
"This animal is a horse," said Lone Owl.
"I have seen them before.
The paleface men brought them here.
They ride on their horses' backs.
Quick, Wolf Cub. We must hide!
The paleface men may be near."

Lone Owl and Wolf Cub hid
behind a pile of rocks,
where they could watch
without being seen.

Chapter 4
STARFIRE

They waited a long time
while Estrella stayed nearby,
eating grass.
No paleface men came.
At last Lone Owl said,
"A horse would be of great use
to our people. We have never had
such an animal."

"Let me go to her, Father,"
begged Wolf Cub.
"She will not harm me."
Lone Owl watched his son
walk slowly toward the horse.

Lone Owl kept his bow ready,
just in case.
But when Estrella saw Wolf Cub
walking toward her,
she came to meet him.

The boy and the golden horse stood
side by side for a long time.

"See, Father, she is my friend,"
cried Wolf Cub.
"Then you must name her, my son."
"She already has a name,"
said Wolf Cub.
"It is Starfire."

At dawn, Wolf Cub climbed gently
onto Starfire's back.
Lone Owl raised his bow again.
But the horse stood still.
Wolf Cub held on to her long mane.
Starfire began walking slowly forward.

With her head held high,
Starfire carried Wolf Cub
over the hill and
down the long trail
to the place where his people lived.

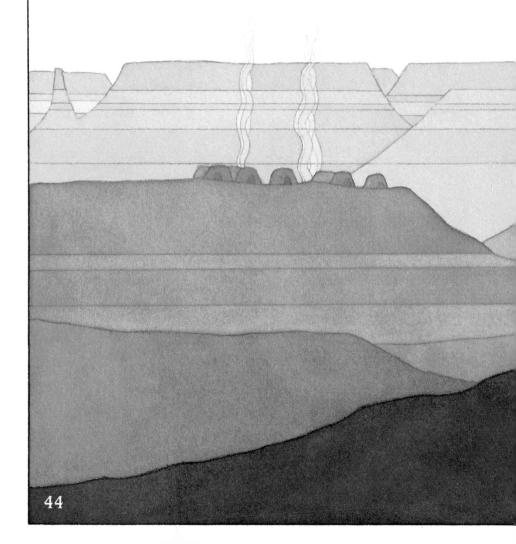